MiLO

Imagines the World

words by Matt de la Peña
Newbery Medal-winning author

pictures by Christian Robinson
Caldecott Honor-winning illustrator

What begins as a slow, distant glow
grows and grows
into a tired train that clatters down the tracks.
A cool rush of wind quiets into a screech of steel,
and when the doors slide open, Milo slips aboard.

The train bucks back into motion
as he and his sister squeeze onto bench seats.
The whiskered man beside Milo has a face of concentration.
A businessman has a blank, lonely face.

The wedding-dressed woman near the far door
has a face made out of light,
while the dog peeking out of her handbag has no face at all,
just a long, lolling tongue.

These monthly Sunday subway rides
are never ending, and as usual, Milo is a shook-up soda.
Excitement stacked on top of worry
on top of confusion
on top of love.
To keep himself from bursting, he studies
the faces around him and makes pictures of their lives.

At a downtown local stop, the whiskered man folds up his crossword and hurries off the train.

Milo imagines him trudging
through brown mounds of slush.
It's a five-flight climb
to his cluttered apartment,
where he's greeted by mewling cats
and burrowing rats.

Parakeets tweet songs of longing
as the man sips tepid soup,
hunched over a game of solitaire.

Late that night,
the door to the parakeet cage
mysteriously falls open,
and the cats gather on the cold sill
to watch the birds fly free above the city.

Milo tugs his sister's sleeve and holds up his picture.

But even when she turns to look, he can tell she doesn't see.

She's a shook-up soda, too.

A boy in a suit boards the train with his dad.
His hair is a perfect part, and there's not a single scuff
on his bright white Nikes.

Milo imagines the *clop clop clop*
of the horse-drawn carriage
that will carry him to his castle.

Imagines the *clink clink clink*
of the guards slowly lowering the drawbridge.

Across the human-made moat
the boy is met by a butler, two maids,
and a gourmet chef offering
crust-free sandwich squares.

Milo flips to a fresh page at a bustling Midtown stop.
When the wedding-dressed woman strides off the train,
a band of street performers launches into "Here Comes the Bride,"
and everyone on the platform stops and cheers.

Milo imagines
the grand cathedral ceremony
where the couple will be pronounced
husband and wife.

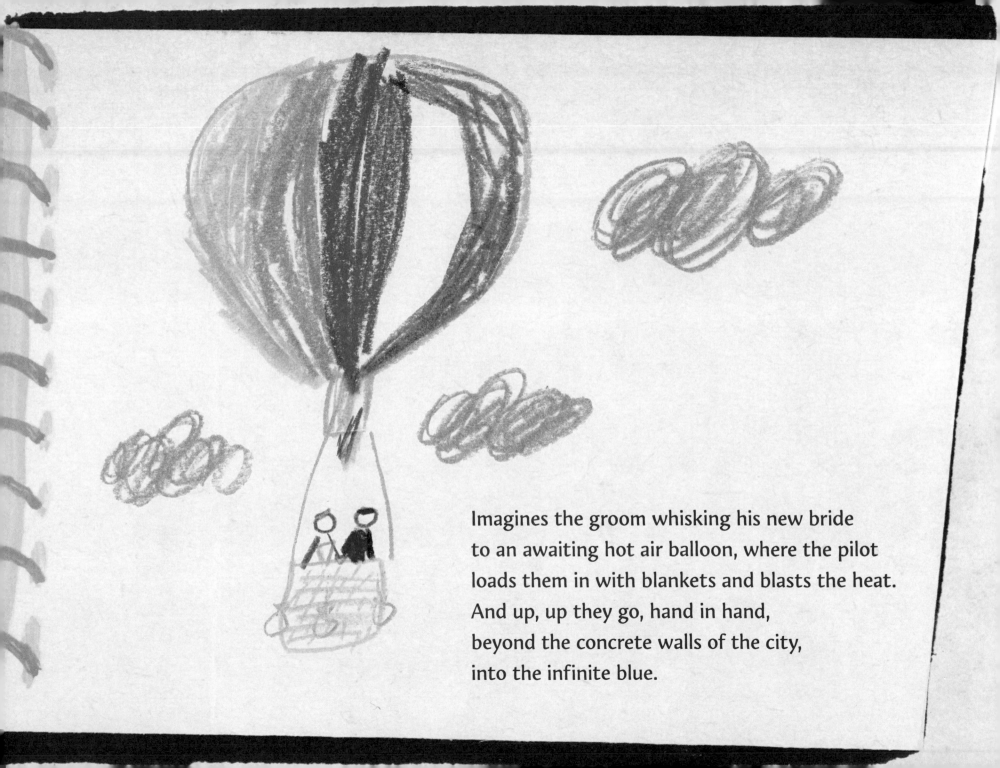

Imagines the groom whisking his new bride
to an awaiting hot air balloon, where the pilot
loads them in with blankets and blasts the heat.
And up, up they go, hand in hand,
beyond the concrete walls of the city,
into the infinite blue.

Milo holds up this picture, too,
but his sister shoos him away.
"Can't you see I'm playing my game?"

He watches her thumbs
bang around her smudged screen,
then turns back to the boy in the suit.

They lock eyes for a few long seconds,
and suddenly it feels like the walls
are closing in around Milo.

The spell is broken when a crew of breakers
bounds onto the train, announcing, "You all ready for a show?"
Several curious faces look up as the beat drops.
And now the girls are walking up walls,

they're whirling around poles,
they're backflipping over shopping bags.
When the train pulls into the next stop,
they collect a few dollars and scramble for another car.

Milo imagines them going from train to train,
doing their act as everyone watches.

But even after the performances are over,
faces still follow their every move.
When they walk down
the electronics aisle
at the department store.

When they cross into the fancy neighborhood.

Milo doesn't really like this picture,
so he puts away his pad and turns
to his reflection in the window.

What do people imagine about *his* face?

Can they see him reciting
his volcano poem to the class?

Can they hear his mom's soothing voice
reading him a bedtime book
over the phone?

Can they smell the chile colorado
bubbling in a pot
in his auntie's apartment
near the cemetery?

Butterflies flood Milo's stomach
when it's finally their stop.
He follows his sister onto the cold station platform
and up the stairs.

Above ground, he's surprised to see
the boy in the suit a few paces ahead.

He's even more surprised when the boy joins the long line
to pass through the metal detector.
Milo's sister suddenly bends to give him a hug.
"I didn't mean to snap at you," she says.
She takes his hand, adding, "You have your picture ready?"
He nods, feeling the warmth of her fingers.

As they slowly shuffle forward,
Milo studies the boy in the suit,
his dad rubbing his thin shoulders.
And a thought occurs to him:
Maybe you can't really know anyone
just by looking at their face.

Milo tries to reimagine all the pictures
he made on the train.
Maybe he could have done it like this instead.

Or this.

Or this.

Milo's chest fills with excitement
when he spots his mom through the crowd.

His sister rushes to give her a hug
before pulling Milo in, too.
And it's in this tight tangle of familiar arms
that he feels most alive.

When they separate, Milo flips through his pad
until he finds the right picture.
"I made this for you," he says, holding it up.
And he watches for the smile
he hopes will spread across his mom's face.

For Miguel de la Peña.
And for those who dare to imagine
beyond a first impression —M. de la P.

For the children, and inner children,
who see themselves in this book —C. R.

G. P. PUTNAM'S SONS
An imprint of Penguin Random House LLC, New York

Text copyright © 2021 by Matt de la Peña
Illustrations copyright © 2021 by Christian Robinson

G. P. Putnam's Sons is a registered trademark of Penguin Random House LLC.

Visit us online at penguinrandomhouse.com

Library of Congress Cataloging-in-Publication Data
Names: de la Peña, Matt, author. | Robinson, Christian, illustrator.
Title: Milo imagines the world / Newbery Medal–winning author Matt de la Peña; Caldecott Honor–winning illustrator Christian Robinson.
Description: New York: G. P. Putnam's Sons, [2021] | Summary: While Milo and his sister travel to a detention center to visit their incarcerated mother, he observes
strangers on the subway and draws what he imagines their lives to be.
Identifiers: LCCN 2020012465 (print) | LCCN 2020012466 (ebook) | ISBN 9780399549083 (hardcover) | ISBN 9780399549090 (ebook) | ISBN 9780399549113 (kindle edition)
Subjects: CYAC: Drawing—Fiction. | Imagination—Fiction. | Prisoners' families—Fiction. | Brothers and sisters—Fiction. | Subways—Fiction.
Classification: LCC PZ7.P3725 Mil 2021 (print) | LCC PZ7.P3725 (ebook) | DDC [E]—dc23
LC record available at https://lccn.loc.gov/2020012465
LC ebook record available at https://lccn.loc.gov/2020012466
Manufactured in China by RR Donnelley Asia Printing Solutions Ltd.
ISBN 9780399549083
1 3 5 7 9 10 8 6 4 2

Design by Eileen Savage | Text set in Amrys
The art was created with acrylic paint, collage, and a bit of digital manipulation.